6/94

COBRA

THE TOTAL PERFORMER!

BY JAY SCHLEIFER

Crestwood House
New York
Maxwell Macmillan Canada
Toronto
Maxwell Macmillan International
New York   Oxford   Singapore   Sydney

Crestwood House
Macmillan Publishing Company
866 Third Avenue
New York, NY 10022

Maxwell Macmillan Canada, Inc.
1200 Eglinton Avenue East
Suite 200
Don Mills, Ontario M3C 3N1

Macmillan Publishing Company is part of the Maxwell Communication
Group of Companies.

First edition

Produced by Twelfth House Productions

Designed by R studio T

Cover photograph courtesy of Ned Scudder

Courtesy of Ned Scudder: 4, 8, 9, 11, 14, 18, 20, 24–25, 26, 29, 31, 34–35, 37, 40–41

Courtesy of the Chrysler Corporation: 44–45, 46

Printed in the United States of America

10 9 8 7 6 5 4 3 2 1

Library of Congress Cataloging-in-Publication Data

Schleifer, Jay.
Cobra / by Jay Schleifer. — 1st ed.
p.   cm.—(Cool classics)
Summary: Discusses the history and dynamics of the vehicle
remembered as one of the finest, purest sports cars ever built.
ISBN 0-89686-701-3
1. Cobra automobile—History—Juvenile literature.   2. Shelby,
Carroll, 1923–   —Juvenile literature.   3. Automobile racing—History—
Juvenile literature. [1. Cobra automobile—History.   2. Shelby, Carroll, 1923–   .]
I. Title.   II. Series.
TL215.C566S35   1993
629.222—dc20   92-14530

CONTENTS

Carroll Shelby created a true dream car in the Cobra.

1 HOW THE COBRA GOT ITS NAME...MAYBE

Carroll Shelby smiled in his sleep. He was dreaming about cars again. As one of the world's top race drivers, Shelby's whole life revolved around cars. So dreaming about them was normal. But the car in the dream wasn't.

At first glance, it looked like one of those cute little English roadsters, like the MG or Austin-Healey. With woodsy dash and skinny wire wheels, it was the sort of car driven by gents wearing tweed sweaters and bow ties.

But something was very different about this English sports car. Its stance on the road was lower than usual, and its tires were fatter than most. The car's body was stretched tight over the tires. It looked like a bodybuilder trying to button his shirt over a bulging chest.

At the rear, the usual soda-straw-sized exhaust pipe was nowhere to be seen. Instead, two fire-hose-sized exhaust pipes poked from under the sides. The pipes hinted strongly that there was something very special under the hood. And what came from those pipes gave you an even better clue. It was the BRATTTTTT-BRATTTTTTT machine-gun-like blast of a big American V-8 engine.

*The performance of the car matched the sound. Instead of the polite zip of most English cars, this beast ate the road alive! It went from zero to 60 mph in less than five seconds, with only a cloud of tire smoke to mark its passing. It reached 100 mph in just a few seconds more. And when the driver locked on the **disk brakes,** the car stopped on the spot. Incredible!*

Suddenly Shelby saw who was driving this major motion ma-

chine. He was, of course. He was wearing his famous bib overalls, his black cowboy hat and a smile as wide as his home state of Texas. He had good reason to smile. Carroll Shelby had invented this amazing car by stuffing a big Ford V-8 engine into a lightweight English A. C. roadster. What's more, he'd soon put his delicious mix on sale at Ford dealers across the United States. Only one thing was missing—the car needed a name to match its special brand of excitement.

Now as the car in the dream got closer, it suddenly turned and roared toward Shelby. For the first time, he noticed some writing on its hood: Cobra.

Years later Carroll Shelby said the name Cobra came to him in a dream. Some people said that Shelby made up the dream to make people remember the car better. If so, he needn't have bothered. Whatever he named it, the car he built would always be remembered as one of the finest, purest sports cars ever. The Cobra was built for 100 percent sports performance. This is its story.

 THE OLD SNAKE CHARMER

The idea of stuffing an American V-8 engine into a lightweight sports-car body is not new. Many carmakers tried it before Carroll Shelby, and all of them failed. It took a special breed of car builder to make the idea happen. The builder had to be a car expert, speed freak, business leader and showman. Slow-talking, fast-driving Carroll Shelby was all of these and more.

Shelby came from Texas, and he liked to remind people of that fact. He was born in a little town near Dallas on January 11, 1923. Shelby's father was a mailman, his mother a homemaker.

As Shelby grew up, so did the age of the gasoline engine. And it wasn't long before Shelby was bitten by the speed bug. By the time Shelby got to high school he was a car buff. He often hung out at the local dirt track to watch the jalopies race. He got his diploma. But he also learned about the nuts and bolts of automobiles.

Years later, Shelby's interest in cars led him to a friend who owned a little English MG sports car. The spindly MG nipped in and out of traffic like a dog running between the legs of horses on parade. One day in May 1952, the friend offered Shelby a chance to try the car in a race. To the friend's amazement—and Shelby's—the 29-year-old Texan won his heat the first time out! Then Shelby took the car out in the next heat, against stiffer competition, and won again! Two wins in his first two sports-car races! For Carroll Shelby, chicken ranching would never be the same.

Shelby's spectacular driving was noticed by other car owners. Before long people wanted him to drive better and better machines. By the mid-1950s, Shelby was a local legend.

That legend was about to become larger—or at least more unusually dressed! One hot day, Shelby was working at his ranch and forgot he was due at a race that same afternoon. By the time he remembered, it was too late to put on his driving suit. Shelby had to pilot his sports machine in the same bib overalls he wore to feed the roosters and hens. As usual, he won. And he quickly became known as the fastest chicken rancher on wheels.

Carroll Shelby was a real showman. To prove it, he began wearing the bib overalls regularly. He even added a cowboy hat to emphasize the Texas good-old-boy look. The crowds loved it! And the offers to drive got better and better.

Shelby drove on the American racing circuit for a couple of years. Then he was discovered by managers of important interna-

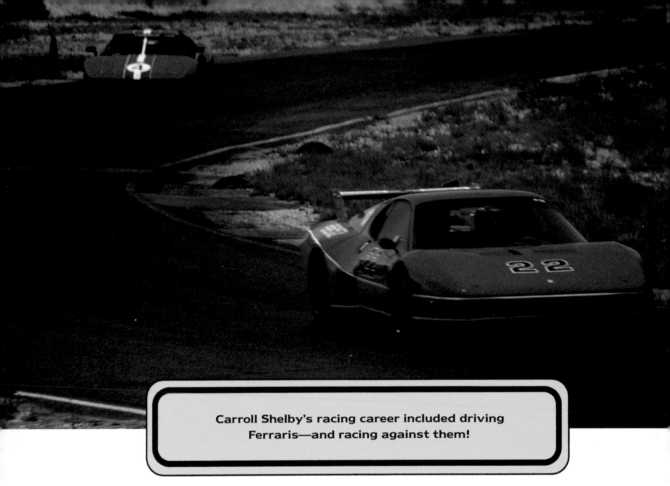

Carroll Shelby's racing career included driving Ferraris—and racing against them!

tional racing teams. These managers saw how fast this funny-looking, funny-sounding farmer really was.

Within a few years, the farmer from Texas was living in Italy, driving Ferraris and Maseratis. He was running wheel to wheel with the world's best drivers.

While Shelby enjoyed the great cars of Europe, he noticed one thing. European sports cars were state-of-the-art in racing, but their engines weren't much more powerful than the good old American V-8s of his hot-rod days back in Texas. The difference was in the weight. European cars were lighter. Shelby thought it would be great to race a lightweight car with American V-8 power.

8

In June 1959, Shelby's major race was the famous 24 hours of Le Mans. Le Mans is a 24-hour race, often run in rain and fog. It's well known for destroying cars and sometimes drivers. This endless, punishing race demands top performance.

At the time of the 1959 Le Mans, Shelby was driving for Aston-Martin. He knew that the race would be a battle of Astons against Ferraris from start to finish. He also knew that the red-hot Italian cars were up to 20 mph faster in the straights. He could only hope that the Astons were stronger and could outlast Enzo Ferrari's best.

When the race was finally run, Shelby and his co-driver dogged the leading Ferrari lap after lap and hour after hour. As night turned to day, it looked like Ferrari would win. Then suddenly, in

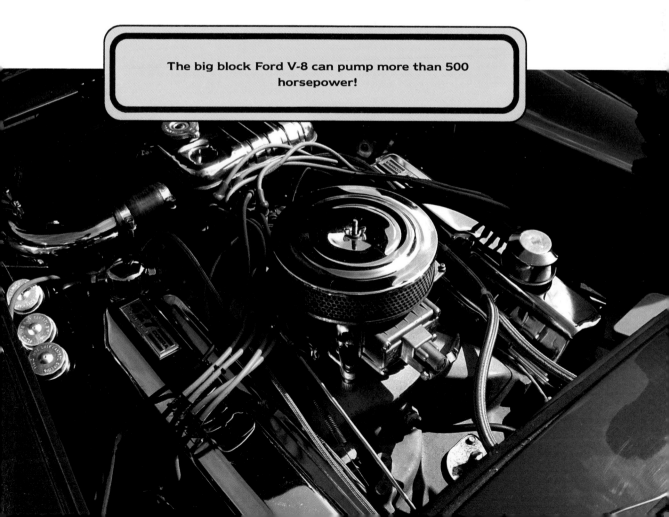

The big block Ford V-8 can pump more than 500 horsepower!

the last moments, Shelby heard the Ferrari's engine begin to fail. If only he could hold on a little longer....

When the checkered flag finally fell, Shelby had beaten the odds—and the Italians. With his co-driver, the one-time hot rodder had won the world's greatest race!

In the fall of 1960, Shelby began having severe chest pains. Carroll Shelby had a weak heart. If he continued to race, he risked a heart attack and maybe death. The famous bib overalls and cowboy hat had to be hung up as far as racing was concerned. But Shelby was only 37. What would he be able to do with the rest of his life?

3 A. C. + FORD = ???

If this were 1960 and you were into cars, there'd be one place you'd want to live: southern California. With its year-round warmth, sunny beaches and winding canyon roads, the area around Los Angeles was sports-car heaven. That's just where Shelby headed.

He hadn't been a racing superstar long enough to save much money. Luckily, his fame opened some doors. He was chosen to sell Goodyear racing tires in the area. He opened a driving school. And he did some work for a local sports-car magazine. None of this made Shelby rich. But it paid well enough for him to think about more than where the next meal would come from.

One thought that came again and again was the idea he had for a lightweight car powered by an American V-8 engine. Shelby was especially interested in the Chevrolet V-8, the advanced engine of the time. He wrote Chevy a letter, offering to build such a car for them if they would pay for it. Chevy's answer was thanks,

but no thanks.

**The first Cobra was based on the English A.C. Ace.
This Cobra is painted in British Racing Green.**

Then, through his contacts at the car magazine, Shelby got two bits of important news. To most people the information didn't seem connected at all. But to Shelby, they merged to create an explosion of excitement.

First, he heard that the Ford Motor Company was about to build an extremely advanced 221-**cubic-inch** V-8 for a new car called the Fairlane. The engine would be built with **thin-wall construction,** a way of making engines lighter without losing power. The Ford Fairlane was a family car, but Shelby felt that the V-8 engine would be perfect for a sports machine. Later, Ford enlarged the engine to 260 cubic inches, then to 289 cubic inches. That made it even better!

Second, Shelby heard that an English sports-car maker named A. C. Cars, Limited, was about to *lose* its supplier of engines. A. C. was too small a firm to have its own engine factory. So it had been powering its sports car, called the Ace, with a six-cylinder engine made by another company called Bristol. But Bristol was moving on to other work and would no longer make engines.

From his days in Europe, Shelby knew the Ace well. It had the look and feel of an English sports car. But it also had a raciness that cars like the MG or Triumph lacked. That was because some of its lines came right off the early-model Ferraris.

More important was the Ace's **chassis.** The car's frame was a sturdy ladder design. There were disk brakes all around. And all four wheels were hung from the frame separately, by a system called **independent suspension.** That meant each wheel could handle a bump in the road without the other wheels being affected.

In comparison, most other English sports cars used **solid-axle suspension** in the rear. The wheels were rigidly connected by a beam of metal. When one rear wheel hit a bump, the other was lifted along with it. With the entire rear end bouncing up and down on every bump, handling suffered.

Because of its fine chassis, the Ace was a strong performer even with the wimpy Bristol six-cylinder engine. With American V-8 power, Shelby knew it had the makings of a superstar!

Shelby had to work fast! He contacted both A. C. and Ford with his idea. He told A. C. that he would be willing to buy fully built, engineless Aces from them. Then he'd buy the new Ford V-8 and stuff it under the hood. This matchup would create the most rip-roaring sports car either England or America had ever seen!

12   While the plan seemed brilliant, Shelby knew it had problems.

He had no factory in the United States to assemble the cars. He had no dealers to sell and repair them. And he didn't have the money to start a business. He only had his idea, his fame as a racer and the guts to try to make it happen.

Ford answered Shelby first. Unbelievably, they were interested! Shelby had stumbled in at exactly the right time.

Ford was about to build the Mustang—the first affordable sporty car. To help sales, the company was pushing the idea of "total performance" in its advertising. And to give the writers a story to tell in their ads, Ford had jumped into racing! Ford stock cars, backed by factory help, were becoming the kings of **NASCAR.** Work had begun on a Ford-powered Indy 500 machine. The company was also interested in becoming a major power in sports cars, where archrival Corvette was the big name. Ford was willing to supply engines, money and other help if they found the right partner—someone who could hold up his end of the deal.

To Ford, Shelby seemed like that partner. But their desire to do business with him was built on a misunderstanding! Ford had somehow gotten the idea that Shelby was some kind of Texas cattle millionaire. They thought he could easily put up the cash for his part of the deal. In reality, Shelby had barely a spare dollar.

Armed with Ford's offer, Shelby sped off to England to meet with the Hurlock brothers, owners of A. C. Cars. He didn't have a problem getting *their* interest. The Ace probably would have died without Shelby. If Ford would ship an engine, said the Hurlocks, they'd shoehorn it into an Ace and try to make the thing work.

The task was easier said than done! Part after part that worked just fine with the Bristol six-cylinder was torn to shreds by the powerful V-8.

All through January 1962 the Hurlock brothers and their nephew Derek labored to find the right mix of parts. On February 1 the **13**

The Old Snake Charmer himself, Carroll Shelby.

CSX0001 (Carroll Shelby Experimental Number 1) rolled out of the little A. C. factory. It was bare metal, without even a paint job. But Carroll Shelby settled in, fastened his seat belt and keyed his creation to life.

It was probably like the day that Frankenstein's monster first stepped out of the castle. The engine's roar, usually muffled by acres of sedan metal, blasted right through the light aluminum skin of the sports car. The car took off like a jackrabbit and never ran out of go. Until Shelby hit the four big disk brakes, that is. Then it stopped *right away*! The handling was pretty slick too.

Shelby stepped out, grinning from ear to ear. He had a winner, all right. He quickly arranged to have the car shipped back to California.

 ## THE SNAKE PIT

What makes a great car? It's not huge factories and thousands of workers. The big car companies have those. They spend billions of dollars and produce hundreds of new designs a year. Yet most are forgotten as fast as there are new ones to replace them.

What really makes a great car is a powerful automotive idea and talented, dedicated people to make it happen. Shelby had the idea. Now he needed the people.

He didn't have to look far. The sports-car, hot-rod and drag-racing clubs of southern California were crawling with car builders. And Shelby had some talented people at his fingertips at the Shelby Performance Driving School. There he found 24-year-old Pete Brock, the perfect candidate for designer.

Brock had wanted to be a car designer since childhood. He could draw cars, and he knew how to create designs that worked **15** when built. He'd been talented enough to get a job at GM in Detroit as a trainee designer. But GM's big-company rules had felt like a noose around his neck. And Brock had broken free to return to the California sun.

When Brock heard about the Cobra (by now, Shelby had named the car), he jumped at the chance to work on it. Since the body had already been designed by A. C., Brock took on all the other jobs that needed an artist's touch. He created the car's snakelike badge and the advertising art. He also designed the CS logo, which looked like a racetrack map and stood for Shelby's initials.

Phil Remington came next. Remington was a race tuner and car builder who'd learned his art the hard way, with a set of wrenches and plenty of skinned knuckles. Besides being good at his job, he brought something special to the company—a factory! Remington had already spent years working for a rich young man who also dreamed of building an American-powered race winner. That young man had gone on to other things. But he left behind an equipped factory in Venice, California. That's where Remington worked. And the two came as a package deal! The package soon included Ken Miles and Al Dowd, two more racers who would become car testers and all around go-getters.

Ford sent Ray Geddes, a young lawyer and accountant who took over the young company's money matters. Geddes freed Shelby from the firm's pocketbook. Now he was able to spend all his time worrying about making the car right. And he was good at that!

The factory, nicknamed the Snake Pit, was just the right size and had just the right tools. But it lacked a test track and Ford was not about to buy one for Shelby.

Fortunately, it didn't matter. "We had a nice curving road

around the apartment houses at nearby Marina del Rey," recalls Al Dowd. "And we knew all the cops out there. Every car we sold out of the Venice plant was tested on that road."

With a factory and car-building team in place, Shelby needed a car-selling team—dealers to sell and service the new machine. A group of specially chosen Ford dealers was signed on. But signing them was just the first step. The salespeople normally sold family sedans. They had to be trained to deal with sports cars and sports-car buyers. The job training fell to Peyton Cramer, another young expert sent by Ford.

As the Cobra team came together, it became clear that Shelby had something working for him. It was something that others who had tried to follow the same dream didn't have. His new company combined the street smarts of the California hot rodders, the sports-car experience of the English *and* the money of giant Ford Motor Company.

Of course, the three didn't always get along. A small battle over the car's name showed that. Everyone agreed Cobra was a wonderful choice for this quick, new road warrior. But Shelby wanted to call it the Shelby Cobra, the Hurlocks wanted it called the A. C. Cobra, and Ford, of course, wanted it to be Ford Cobra. Finally a deal was worked out. The car would be the Shelby Cobra in America and the A. C. Cobra in England. But in both places it would carry a red, white and blue badge that read "Powered by Ford." It was lucky that both the United States and British flags are red, white and blue!

Then, when it seemed like all was settled, someone discovered that the name Cobra itself might belong to someone else! In the 1950s another car builder had come up with a new way of making engines called "COpper BRAzing," and he'd used the Cobra name on his engines. If the builder still had rights to the name,

Here's a shot of an early small block Cobra. They don't get more classic than this!

Shelby would have to go back to square one—or else have another dream!

Ford's lawyers studied the matter while everyone waited in anticipation. Finally, the decision came: By going out of the car business, the maker had given up all rights to the name. It was Shelby's for the taking. Now, finally, only one thing was missing— the car itself. Soon it was on its way from England!

5 WINNING WITH A WINNER!

The Cobra's first "competition" in America would be at the 1962 New York Auto Show. The show was like a giant coming-out party for new cars. Every maker displayed its new street machines and dream cars. The crowds were huge, and they included writers for all the major car magazines. If the writers noticed the Cobra among the hundreds of beautiful machines, the car would become famous practically overnight.

For the show, Shelby had the CSX0001 finished off with a screaming yellow paint job and chrome wire wheels. Competitors surrounded their cars with pretty models and even musical shows. Shelby let the Cobra stand alone. But he got lucky when the car was placed right near the entrance to the area. The Cobra was one of the first cars people saw.

Many people never got much farther. The car was like a magnet, drawing huge crowds. "Everyone just knew it could suck the headlights out of anything else in the building," one writer said. "The thing looked like it was going 150 mph just sitting there."

The auto show was a huge success for Shelby. And it was a good thing that the show lasted less than a week. There was something wrong with the car's paint job. The gorgeous yellow paint turned to pink, white and rusty brown! The whole car had to be repainted!

Overnight, a new car star was born. It was written about in major magazines all over America. Now it was time to see if the Cobra's lunge was up to its looks. Racing season had begun. The next round of competition would be at 150 miles an hour.

The round began in the Cobra's backyard at a three-hour event at the track in Riverside, California. By this time, a second

19

car had been delivered by A. C. and it got the full racing treatment. It had a cut-down windshield, extra air vents for the engine, a roll bar to protect the driver in a rollover crash, and fat side exhaust pipes that made slightly less noise than World War II artillery. Actually, the changes were minor since the Cobra was a race car from the very beginning. This was a total sports car. Going fast was its main mission in life.

The Cobra is a serious road machine, from the bare cabin to the racing seatbelts.

When the Cobra hit the track, Shelby was delighted to see that the car he was running against was the new Corvette Sting Ray. He probably remembered writing to Chevy and being told they didn't need his help. Today he'd see if they did.

From the green flag, it was clear the Cobra could more than hold its own. The rapid little roadster roared past the leading Vette and kept on widening the lead. Soon the Cobra was on its own, more than a mile and a half out front and bound to win. Then a part broke, putting the car on the sidelines. Luckily, the car was easy to fix. Next time the Cobra and Vette met, the result would probably be different.

The next race was outside the United States, at Nassau in the Bahama Islands. Vettes were there, but this time, so were Europe's biggest names: Ferrari, Maserati, Lotus and Porsche. Could the Cobra top the world's best? Would Shelby's belief that an American V-8 could run with supercars hold up in battle? Again, the Cobra looked sharp at the start and threatened to run away with the race. But at a fuel stop, someone goofed on the amount of fuel the car needed and the powerful V-8 soon putt-putted to a stop. That someone was Shelby himself, working the fuel cans in the pits. He'd only filled one of the car's two tanks. It was a dumb way to lose, especially for one of the world's top racers! But once again the cure was easy.

 SMOOTHING OUT THE BRICK

Over the next two years—1963 and 1964—the Cobra exploded like dynamite on U.S. racetracks. But the car was a bust in the rest of the racing world. The reasons are easy to understand.

In the United States, the Cobra ran in local events put on by the Sports Car Club of America and other U.S. racing groups. Their tracks were usually short and full of curves. On these kinds of tracks, Shelby's snake wiggled around at its best. Also, the other cars were usually entered by private owners. No major factory teams showed up for these local events. And while the private owners ran Ferraris and other top machines, they didn't have the dollars or knowledge to beat the Cobra.

The biggest threat Shelby faced was the new 1963 Corvette Sting Ray. The Vette had a bigger engine and was more technologically advanced than Shelby's A. C.–Ford half-breed. But it was also heavier. Keeping things light paid off again and again. Against the Cobras, the Vettes were usually left in the dust.

In overseas races, the story was different. There the Cobras faced top factory teams. Shelby was running against the best that Enzo Ferrari and his experts could deliver. What's more, the tracks were longer, with straights that went on and on. The straight at Le Mans, for example, is three miles long! A powerful car could reach almost 200 mph!

Tracks like that favored cars with awesome top speeds, not nimble handlers like the Cobra. Shelby's snakes would surge through the turns at the front of the pack. But then the Ferraris would simply run away from them in the long straights.

The problem with the Cobra was its bricklike shape. No matter how much power Shelby punched out of the Ford V-8, his cars weren't going any faster without a more streamlined body. At about 160 mph, the Cobras seemed to hit a wall of air. Ferrari's slinky GTO coupe would then slide by on its way to 180 or better. With a 20-mph edge in top speed, the Ferrari driver could practically sit down for a bowl of pasta before the Cobra showed up to challenge him again!

The answer: Someone had to reshape the Cobra's blunt body. They'd have to build a slinky new coupe body over the already excellent chassis. That someone was designer Pete Brock. Brock had to smooth out the brick!

The car began with nothing more than a sketch on the wall. The drawing showed a long, low-nosed animal with wildly upswept tail and a huge sheet of rear window.

Following the shapes in Brock's drawings, workers cut wooden boards and made them into a kind of skeleton. The boards looked like the frame of a model airplane before the skin is attached. This was then bolted onto a Cobra roadster chassis.

Next, master body builders beat large sheets of metal over the skeleton with hammers, bending them into the shape of the car's skin. Windows, door hinges, lights and other parts were made or bought and installed. And finally, the body was painted in a gorgeous blue paint job with wide white racing stripes—the official racing colors of the United States.

The car was a stunner. But its design was smart as well as beautiful. Phil Remington saw to that. Remington, Shelby's top engineer, had joined the act and added his ideas. For example, he built air tubes into the bodywork. When the car ran fast, lots of fresh air was delivered right to the radiator. This drew heat from the engine. Then the hot air flowed out through a vent on top of the hood.

Neither Brock nor Remington made a single blueprint to guide the process. And in fact, each time another coupe was made, the car came out different. Six coupes were made. No two were exactly alike!

Finally, the day came to test the new super Cobra. The car was trucked out to a deserted road and fired up. And the faster the driver pushed it, the faster it rolled. A speed of 160 came and went

The Cobra had the power to keep up with Ferraris,
but its brick-like shape slowed it down.

easily, with lots of throttle left. The coupe's slick body was slicing through the air like a sharp knife. The car had a top speed of 180 or better. The Ferraris that ran that fast were now well within reach! Thanks to Brock and Remington, the Cobra now had a body that stood up to the power of its chassis.

When it first ran, the car was known simply as the Cobra coupe. But the first race it ran was at Daytona, Florida, so reporters began to call it the Cobra Daytona. The name stuck. Pretty soon it became known all over the world.

Pete Brock's Daytona coupe body increased the Cobra's top speed by more than 20 mph!

7 **THAT CHAMPIONSHIP SEASON**

In the world of big-time motor racing, there's never been a time like the mid-1960s. This was when the most famous name in racing, Ferrari, was challenged by one of the biggest auto companies in the world, Ford. It was war out there. Ferrari's endless experience was battling against Ford's endless resources.

Top Ford executives looked around for a head start. They didn't have to look far. They were already tied in with a top racer. He was a wily Texan named Carroll Shelby. And he was already building a Ford-powered race car in California.

Shelby was thrilled. He had the perfect weapons: the classic Cobra and the brand-new Daytona Coupe. After a while, he also had a special all-out racer called the GT-40 that Ford had created on its own. Ford handed over these cars to him and asked him to run them. It was time to get into big-time racing!

The 1963 and 1964 seasons were building years. The Shelby team tested their cars again and again. They had wins, but they also had lots of losses. Something was always breaking. They'd fix it, and then send the news to the California factory so the rest of the cars could get the same repair. The cars were constantly improved. In time they became as reliable as freight trains, and a whole lot faster.

The prize everyone was after was the World Manufacturer's Championship for GT cars. It went to the top car factory in racing each year.

During the 1950s and early 1960s, Enzo Ferrari practically owned the Manufacturer's Championship. His wild red cars would go out and win it year after year. It seemed like the other cars were extras in a movie that Ferrari had written, directed, and starred in. **27**

They never had a chance. But Carroll Shelby was not willing to be an extra.

The 1965 season was a seesaw battle. Shelby won the GT class in the first major race at Daytona, Florida, with a Daytona Coupe. Then he followed that win with one at Sebring, another famous Florida racetrack.

From there, the series moved to Europe. Ferrari did better in its own backyard, but the Cobras still looked unbeatable. In June, even though Ferrari scored an overall win at the famous 24-hour race at Le Mans, France, the American cars took their class. Championship points were piling up. Finally Shelby got his chance to clinch the title—a race at the ultra-high-speed track at Reims, France.

At races like this, Pete Brock's streamlined styling really paid off. The Cobra Daytonas, wearing California license plates, slithered up the straight at speeds of 180 mph. A Daytona won its class, and another cruised in right behind it in second place. This one-two punch finished Ferrari for the year. Cobra, the little company owned by a former chicken farmer, had clinched the 1965 World Manufacturer's Championship.

 **THE SUPER COBRA**

Every Cobra you've read about until now, including the Daytona Coupe, was powered by Ford's lightweight V-8. The engine, which also powered millions of family cars, started out at 221 cubic inches. Then it was enlarged to 260. In the Cobras, it was an even bigger 289. Later it grew to 302 inches to become the famous "5.0 **liter** V-8" which is well known in the recent Mustang GT.

The Daytona Coupe helped Carroll Shelby clinch the
1965 World Manufacturer's Championship.

Each time the small V-8 was enlarged, it became more powerful. But every engine has its limit. The **small block**'s limit was about 400 horsepower. Shelby experts couldn't get more horses out of the small-block barn without breaking the engine.

Shelby knew he had to have more. Ferrari ran V-12 engines, which could break the 400 horsepower barrier with ease. Corvette started with a small block. But before long, Chevy engineers squeezed a big 377-inch engine into the Sting Ray, and followed that with even larger engines. The Cobra's light weight still gave Shelby his edge. But that couldn't last. He needed more power. And he needed it fast!

Luckily, Shelby knew where he could get it. Ford had another engine, one that was spoken of in quiet whispers and with great respect. It was the monster, the superweapon, the one people knew would turn the Cobra into King Kong—if it could be made to work. It was Ford's **big block** 427-cubic-inch V-8.

Developed for NASCAR stock-car races, the 427 boasted more than 400 horsepower. It also looked and felt like a monster. It weighed more than four grown men. Shelby knew that the 427 could pump close to 500 horsepower if it had to. But he also knew that the little car A. C. had built for a six-cylinder would never hold up under the stampede. That kind of power would tear it to shreds.

Still, it was worth a try.

The first attempt was made in late 1963. Shelby mechanics pulled a small block out of a hapless Cobra chassis lying around in the shop. Then they lowered a 427 into its place. Amazingly, the engine fit, but there wasn't much room to spare. Now changes were made so the engine could be locked in place. Then the car was taken out to a test track for a very, *very* careful first drive.

The mismatch didn't take long to show up. The big beast ran hot, and there was no room in the small body for cooling air to calm it

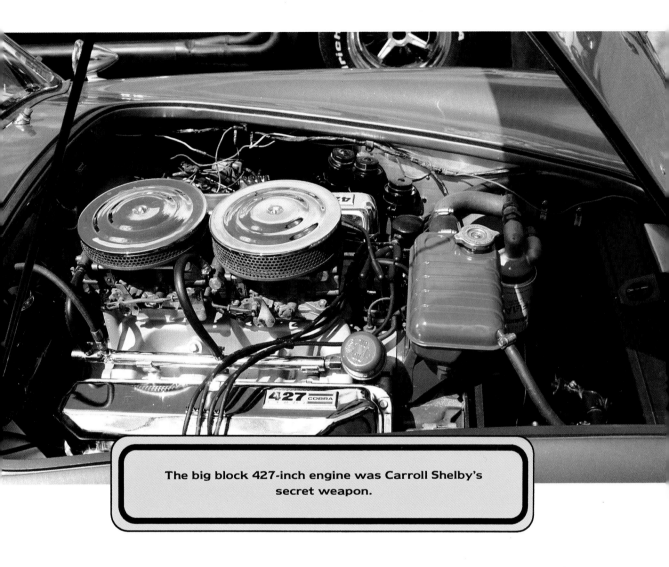

The big block 427-inch engine was Carroll Shelby's secret weapon.

down. Before long, the cockpit was so overheated that the driver's shoe was sticking to the gas pedal. Plus, even the short drive showed that the big engine was too much for other parts of the car like springs and brakes. The car staggered under the load. But it staggered with incredible speed, and the noise the thumping engine made in the thin body was loud enough to wake up people miles away. The Shelby crew looked at each other and grinned.

This would be worth doing right!

In fact, a completely new design was called for. The 427 Cobra would look something like the original model. And its body would still be made by A. C. in England. But it really would be a totally new car.

The Ford connection really paid off with the new car. Shelby's small band of former hot rodders suddenly had all Ford's computer power at their fingertips. Need to know how much metal should go into the springs? No problem, the computer told all! Want to know what size tires would work best? The computer knew. Ford's computers saved thousands of hours of testing. The result was a better car.

The biggest changes from the original Cobra were in the size and the spring system. The new supersnake was beefier in every way. It was longer and much wider. Fat tires were covered with fat **wheel flares.** A larger snout let more cooling air into the engine. And in case anyone didn't notice the other changes, a pair of dumper exhausts as wide as sewer pipes ran down each side.

The original car had **leaf-spring suspension**, the system that's used on horse-drawn wagons. These were replaced by coil springs, a more modern method of springing. And brakes, steering and other key parts were made stronger. A heavy bomber was taking the place of the original fighter jet.

The small V-8 car had been able to run rings around the competition. The big block machine would flatten them!

On the other hand the car went from zero to 60 mph in under four seconds. And top speeds were over 180 mph—even with the brick-shaped body! The power of the giant engine could lay rubber for blocks, snap your neck back and paint your seat-belt buckle onto your belly button!

Shelby built only about 350 of these monsters, some with a

slightly larger 428-cubic-inch engine. But they remain the last word in Cobra excitement. And every one still around today is collector's gold—worth as much as a half-million dollars!

 TRAMPLED BY MUSTANGS

By the time the 427 Cobras roamed the earth, big changes had happened at Shelby's Snake Pit. It was getting hard to tell where Shelby's company ended and Ford began. The little band of hot rodders that built the Cobra CSX0001 was being eaten whole by the giant from Detroit.

The change came with the Mustang G.T.-350 project.

Early in 1964, Shelby had been called to Detroit to meet none other than Lee Iacocca, then head of Ford. Iacocca was about to introduce the Mustang, and he wanted a special high-performance version to compete against the Corvettes. He asked Shelby to develop and build the car for him.

At first Shelby thought that the task was impossible. As sharp as it looked, the Mustang was little more than a sleek new body over sedan parts. But in time, he found ways to coax performance out of the car. After all, it used the same basic small block V-8 as his Cobra. And the old hot-rod tricks of lightening the body and tightening the springs worked as well as ever. The Shelby Mustang was rough-riding and noisy, but it was also blindingly fast.

To celebrate, Shelby gave each car a gleaming white paint job with broad blue stripes—the opposite of the Cobra, but still official American colors. He called it the G.T. 350. Why? Because it was about 350 feet from his office to a building across the street.

Even without a fancy name, the Shelby Mustang took off in sales. Carroll Shelby had never wanted to build more than a few

Driving a big block Cobra at high speeds requires
both skill and nerve.

hundred Cobras a year. Suddenly he was in the Mustang business, building thousands of cars. His little company had become a big operation.

The money coming in was more than Shelby ever dreamed possible. But he wasn't happy. It just wasn't fun anymore.

Then in late 1966, some of the money people got together and made what's called a "business decision" about the Cobra. They decided to drop it from the lineup. From then on, only Shelby Mustangs would be made.

It seemed the right move at the time. Ford Motor Company was no longer interested in the Cobra. They'd turned their full attention to their racing car, the GT-40. What's more, sales were down. People no longer wanted a loud, hard-riding roadster with an overgrown sedan engine. And all the room at the factory was needed to make those hot-selling Shelby Mustangs. It was good-bye to the car that started it all.

"When push came to shove," says former business manager Peyton Cramer, "something had to go. The Cobra seemed the logical choice."

It was hard to believe, with all that had happened. But it had been only four years since the first Cobra rolled out of Carroll Shelby's dream onto the world's roads. Just over 1,000 had been built. That's as many cars as some factories make each day before lunch. Yet everyone knew the name Cobra and what the car had done.

As part of its deal with Shelby, Ford got the rights to the Cobra name for just one dollar. They've used it over the years on cars that had nothing to do with Shelby. They even pasted the name in giant tape letters on the turtle-slow, mini-Mustang sold during the gas crisis in the 1970s. Some Cobra!

It's a good thing Carroll Shelby wasn't watching. After three

With the G.T. 350, Carroll Shelby took the Ford
Mustang design to new heights of performance.

years of building hot-rod Mustangs for Ford, Shelby finally decided
to hang up his helmet and overalls for good. He went on to many
other things, including running cattle ranches and selling his own
brand of Texas chili—red hot!

You'd probably think the story of the Cobra would end here. But
the Cobra, and Carroll Shelby, still had some surprises to spring
on the motoring world.

⬢ 10 ECHOES OF THUNDER

The young car lover nearly twisted all the way around in his seat. He'd just passed the only gas station in his small town. And there, sitting in the driveway, was what looked like a 427 Cobra. A half-million-dollar collector car right in his hometown! He'd seen pictures of them, sure. But he never expected to see a living legend at the corner of Fifth and Main. Yet there it was, as big as life!

Tossing his Mustang convertible into a wild "180," the car lover hot-rodded it back to the station and slid in sideways, nearly hitting the air pump. Up close, the Cobra was even more amazing. It shined as if it had just been built the day before. Yet the young man knew the last one had been built back in 1966.

Then the car lover began to notice things. The steering wheel looked strangely modern. The radio was 1990s all the way, with tape deck and CD player. And the tires were Goodyear Eagle GT + 4 radials, the same brand as those on his Mustang. This tire didn't exist in 1966.

In a minute, the solution to the mystery became clear. This car was not a Cobra. It was a Repli-Cobra, a copy made with a **fiberglass** *body.*

When you think about it, copying Cobras makes sense. That's why more than a dozen companies do it. All you need to do is borrow one original to make the mold for the body. After that, you can pop off real-looking Cobra bodies as fast as you can lay the fiberglass in the mold.

As for mechanical parts, Ford engines are easy to come by. After all, they are sedan motors! Replica builders use both the small and big block V-8s, and one company even uses a Chevy engine! Other parts can usually be found in one form or another.

Most come off the Ford dealer's shelf or from a junkyard.

The cars sell for anywhere from $20,000 to more than $100,000. The price depends on whether they come ready-built or they need work. Either way, Cobra replicas give people the chance to feel what the real thing was like more than 25 years ago. What's more, with modern parts, Cobra replicas can actually run better and safer than the original. Shelby's car didn't have modern radial tires, engine electronics, pollution controls or **antilock brakes**. The copies do.

But the copies are only part of the continuing Cobra story. Thanks to the Chrysler Corporation and a certain ex-race car driver from Texas, there's an even better way to understand the magic of the Cobra. It's called *Viper*!

In 1982, chili cook and cattle rancher Carroll Shelby had some news that stunned the car world. He'd once again joined his name and his fame with a major U.S. car company. He was going to help them build special models carrying the Shelby name. This time, the company was Chrysler. The move made perfect sense.

After all, the head of Chrysler was Lee Iacocca—the same man who'd backed Shelby when both were involved with Ford. It was Iacocca who'd "invented" the Mustang and asked Shelby to build it into the G.T. 350. Now he needed some of that "Shelby Magic" to add spice to Chrysler's line.

The problem was that Chrysler didn't have Ford's kind of money. So the best Shelby could do at first was help them make a few changes to their sedans and plaster his name across them. But in the back of his mind, Shelby had a dream. And we all know what happens when Carroll Shelby has a dream!

One day in 1988, Shelby flew out to Chrysler headquarters in Detroit to meet with Bob Lutz. Lutz was Chrysler's president—the top man in the company except for Iacocca. Shelby knew Lutz was a

Most Cobra replicas follow the big block design seen here on the Cobra CSX3218.

Cobra lover. Lutz even owned one of the better replicas of the car.

"Wouldn't it be wonderful if you guys could build a 1990s version of the Cobra?" Shelby asked Lutz. "Not a copy, but a brand-new, fully up-to-date car, with the same spirit."

Lutz thought about it. The company was short on cash and down on sales. It was a bad time for the auto industry. But if he let his designers build just one copy for auto shows, there'd be something for them to look forward to at work again. He asked the design team if they wanted to do it.

Chrysler designers were thrilled. Building a modern version of one of the world's top cars was the challenge of a lifetime. They got to work immediately.

In a few short months, an explosive red roadster sat on a turntable at auto shows across America. It was swoopy and rounded, as modern cars are. It looked nothing like the old A. C. brick shape. Yet it had the same kind of "get out of my way" toughness the old car had.

The new car promised more fiery performance than the original Cobra ever had. Instead of a big block V-8, it featured an even *bigger* block 400 horsepower *V-10*. This engine was one of the first ten-cylinder power plants ever used in a modern car. Chrysler had been developing this monstrous engine for a new line of trucks. And with a few changes, it was just the machinery their new road warrior needed to go with its awesome good looks.

Of course, they couldn't call the car Cobra. Ford owned that name. But they did something equally snaky. They named it Viper—Dodge Viper, to be exact.

Just as when the first screaming yellow Cobra appeared, auto show crowds and magazine writers went wild over Shelby's latest road burner. The Viper was seen on car magazine covers nationwide. And letters began to pour into Chrysler headquarters asking when it would be built and what it would cost. Some writers even attached checks as down payments. These were quickly returned. There were no plans to build more than the single show car, Chrysler told the customers. But the blast of interest soon made Bob Lutz wonder if the Viper should indeed be produced.

It was no big deal for Chrysler to build one Viper as a show car. But putting the car into full production was a billion-dollar gamble. And Chrysler was having trouble paying its bills.

For months, company executives had been having the same argument. The business types pushed to spend the time and money on a safer project. The designers and engineers pushed for the Viper. It would be a sign to the world that Chrysler could still duke it out with any carmaker on the road.

In a way, the two groups were arguing about what a car company should be. Was it just a business or was it more?

Lutz finally made the decision, and Iacocca backed him up. Not only would Chrysler build the Viper, it would build it in record time—just three years from idea to showroom. The new Dodge Viper V-10 would roll out in early 1992, the Cobra's 30th birthday.

The plan was to build only a few hundred the first year, then about 5,000 each year after that. This is a small number compared to the 30,000 or more Corvettes built each year, or the hundreds of thousands of copies of cars like the Mustang or the Dodge Daytona. The Viper's price, about $50,000, was reasonable for a supercar. Chrysler knew that even if they sold 5,000 Vipers a year they'd never earn back the millions the car cost to develop. But they planned to put the Viper to another use. Creating the Viper would test a whole new way of building a car.

Usually, the designers do their work first, then hand it over to the engineers. When the engineers finish, they move the car along to the factory to build.

The spirit of the Cobra lives on in the Dodge Viper, a car Carroll Shelby helped design.

It could take up to seven years to get a design from the drawing board to the road using this method. Plus, each group had to do extra work. This is because each group thinks about what they wanted in the car, and not about what other groups wanted. Engineers had to find ways to make the designers' wild lines work as a car. Then the factory had to try to find ways to assemble what the engineers wanted.

For the new sports car, Chrysler created "Team Viper," a mixed group of designers, engineers, factory people and even money and sales specialists. From the first day, they all worked in the same area and talked regularly. .

The final car showed up on schedule, in half the time it usually took to start from scratch. "From now on," said Lee Iacocca, "we'll build all our new cars this way."

Chrysler used a totally new car-building system when it created the Viper.

As soon as the Viper appeared, writers rushed to drive it. They reported the same neck-snapping rush that some hadn't felt since the Cobra CSX0001. The car also had the same ability to stop passersby in their tracks. Even in "car-crazy California" there was a mob scene wherever a Viper showed up. At a snazzy restaurant, one man offered to buy the Viper right on the spot. He just had to have that "wild, red car in the parking lot!"

At age 70, Carroll Shelby was happy with all of this. In the Dodge Viper, the spirit of the Cool Classic called Cobra was alive and well. And he knew that, in one way or another, that spirit would live on forever.

GLOSSARY/INDEX

antilock brakes 39 A braking system on a car designed to keep the wheels from skidding on slippery surfaces.

big block 9, 30, 31, 32, 35, 38, 41, 42 A large V-8 engine, usually more than 350 cubic inches in size.

block 9, 30, 31, 32, 35, 38, 41, 42 The metal core of an engine that houses the major moving parts.

chassis 12, 23, 26, 30 The mechanical parts of the car, including engine, suspension and the frame they are attached to.

coil springs 32 A type of automotive spring using round tubing in a circular shape; resembles a spring shape.

cubic inches 10, 11, 28, 30, 32 A measurement of engine size.

disk brakes 5, 12, 15 A stopping system in which clamps press down on metal disks attached to a car's wheels; especially good in wet weather.

fiberglass 38 A plasticlike material used in car bodies, low in cost and easy to work into unusual shapes; many custom and kit cars are made of fiberglass, as is Chevrolet's Corvette.

independent suspension 12 Attachment of wheels to the chassis in a way that allows all four wheels to soak up bumps separately. Bumps at one wheel do not upset the others.

leaf-spring suspension 32 A means of springing using long, flat metal bars ("leaves") that bend and flex to soak up bumps; used since the days of horse-drawn wagons.

liter 28 Measurement of engine size.

NASCAR 12, 30 National Association of Stock Car Racing. This group makes rules for drag-racing events.

small block 18, 30, 33, 38 A V-8 engine, usually under 350 cubic inches in size.

solid-axle suspension 12 A system of attaching wheels to a car frame, using a solid metal beam to hold each pair of wheels.

supercharger 32 A device that force-feeds gas-air mixture into an engine, greatly increasing its power.

suspension 12, 32 Parts that attach wheels to a car. Usually made to move so they absorb road bumps.

thin-wall construction 11 A way of building engines with less metal than usual, keeping weight down.

wheel flares 32 Parts added to a car's body to cover wider-than-normal tires.